The Happiest Mommy Ever

Written by
Alice Furniss

Illustrations by
Julie Olson

DESERET BOOK

SALT LAKE CITY, UTAH

Text © 2009 Alice Furniss
Illustrations © 2009 Jujubee Illustrations LLC

DESERET BOOK is a registered trademark of Deseret Book Company.

Visit us at DeseretBook.com

Library of Congress Cataloging-in-Publication Data

Furniss, Alice.
  The happiest mommy ever / written by Alice Furniss ; illustrated by Julie Olson.
    p. cm.
  Summary: A mother tells her young son about the happiest times of her life.
  ISBN 978-1-60641-056-1 (hardbound : alk. paper)
  [1. Mothers and sons—Fiction. 2. Happiness—Fiction.] I. Olson, Julie, ill. II. Title.
  PZ7.F96656Hap 2009
  [E]—dc22   2008044536

Printed in the United States of America
Worzalla Publishing Co., Stevens Point, WI

10 9 8 7 6 5 4 3 2 1

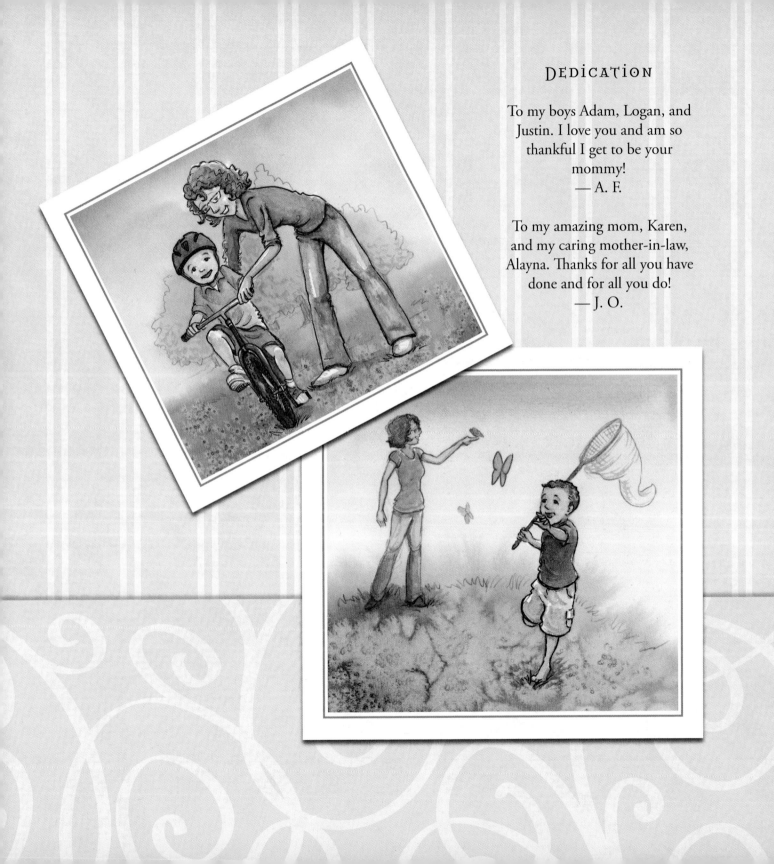

I love my mommy.

Sometimes we make cookies
together, and Mommy will
tell me stories.

One day I asked, "Mommy, what is
the happiest you've ever been?"

"Well," said Mommy, "once when I was just about your age, I was in a dance recital.

PRESENTING

MADAME LEMOND'S LITTLE DANCERS

The Dance of the Flowers
by Little Dancing Class 1

The Dance of the Sugar Plum Fairies
by Little Dancing Class 2

The Dance of the Toy Soldiers
by Little Dancing Boys Class

INTERMISSION

Rockin' Robin
by Little Dancing Class 3

50's Sock Hop
by Little Dancing Class 2 and Little Dancing Boys

Blue Moon
by the Little Ballroom Dancers

Finale
by all the Little Dancing Classes

I danced

and danced

and danced.

And when I was done, the audience clapped and cheered for me. I was so happy!"

"But Mommy, is that the happiest you've EVER been?"

"Well, it *was* until . . .

I grew older and played volleyball
on the school team.

I practiced

and practiced

and practiced.

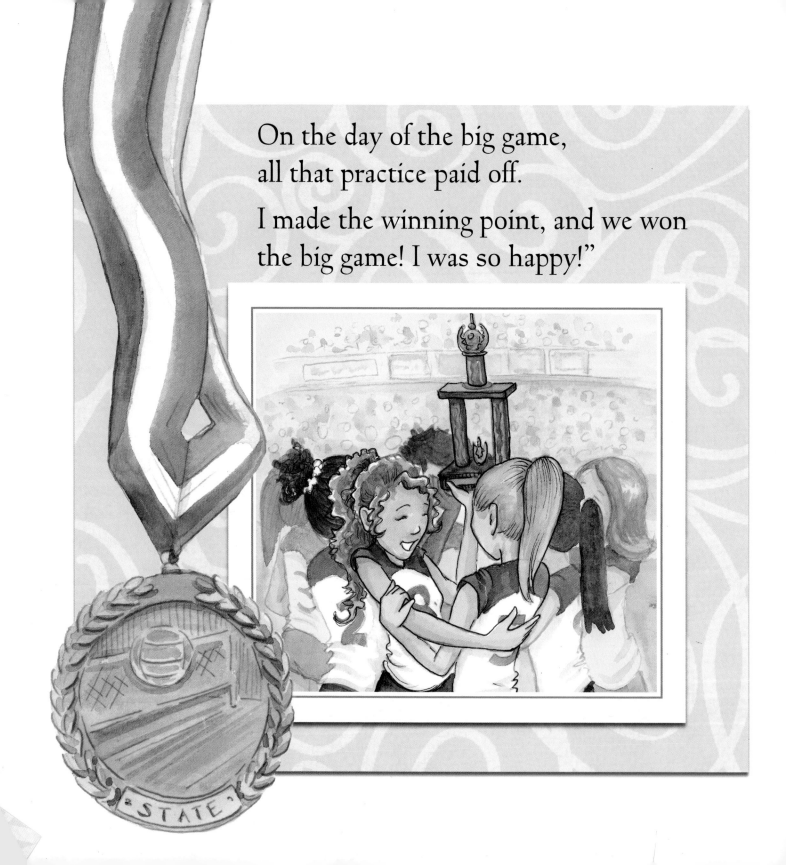

On the day of the big game,
all that practice paid off.

I made the winning point, and we won
the big game! I was so happy!"

"But Mommy, is that the happiest you've EVER been?"

"Well, it *was* until . . .

A few years later, I went off to college.

I studied

and studied

and studied.

After four long years of studying, I graduated and got my college degree.

I was so happy."

"But Mommy, is that the happiest you've EVER been?"

"Well, it *was* until . . .

A few years later, I met your daddy.

We spent lots of time together.

We laughed and

laughed and

laughed.

One day we went to the temple and were married.

All our friends and family were there. I was so happy!"

"But Mommy, is that the happiest you've EVER been?"

"Well, it *was* until . . .

Daddy and I had been married a few years.

We had lots of love in our home and wanted children to share it with.

Then we found out a baby was on the way.

We waited

and waited

and waited.

Finally, our brand-new baby was here.

It was YOU! I was so happy!"

"But Mommy, is that the happiest you've EVER been?"

"Well, it *was* until . . .

A few years later, that little boy
wasn't a baby anymore.

He grew

and grew

and grew.

And then he was a big boy.

A big boy that I love to make
cookies with and tell stories to!

I am so happy!"

"Mommy, is this the happiest you've ever been?"

"Yes, THIS is the happiest I've EVER been!"